Hugh is New

Level 6Ł

Written by Louise Goodman
Illustrated by Keino
Reading Consultant: Betty Franchi

About Phonics

Spoken English uses more than 40 speech sounds. Each sound is called a *phoneme*. Some phonemes relate to a single letter (d-o-g) and others to combinations of letters (sh-ar-p). When a phoneme is written down, it is called a *grapheme*. Teaching these sounds, matching them to their written form, and sounding out words for reading is the basis of phonics.

Early phonics instruction gives children the tools to sound out, blend, and say the words without having to rely on memory or guesswork. This instruction gives children the confidence and ability to read unfamiliar words, helping them progress toward independent reading.

About the Consultant

Betty Franchi is an American educator with a Bachelor's Degree in Elementary and Middle Education as well as a Master's Degree in Special Education. Betty holds a National Boards for Professional Teaching Standards certification. Throughout her 24 years as a teacher, she has studied and developed an expertise in Phonetic Awareness and has implemented phonetic strategies, teaching many young children to read, including students with special needs.

Reading tips

This book focuses on two sounds made with the letter *u*; *(ŭ)* as in b**u**t and p**u**t.

Tricky and/or new words in this book

Any words in bold may have unusual spellings or are new and have not yet been introduced.

> **Tricky and/or new words in this book**
>
> ## Hugh doesn't fruit suits nothing

Extra ways to have fun with this book

After the readers have read the story, ask them questions about what they have just read.

How did Sue get Hugh to play?
Can you remember two words that contain the different u sounds?

Ukulele is as much fun to play as it is to spell.

A Pronunciation Guide

This grid contains the sounds used in the stories in levels 4, 5, and 6 and a guide on how to say them.

/ă/ as in pat	/ā/ as in pay	/âr/ as in care	/ä/ as in father
/b/ as in bib	/ch/ as in church	/d/ as in deed/ milled	/ĕ/ as in pet
/ē/ as in bee	/f/ as in fife/ phase/ rough	/g/ as in gag	/h/ as in hat
/hw/ as in which	/ĭ/ as in pit	/ī/ as in pie/ by	/îr/ as in pier
/j/ as in judge	/k/ as in kick/ cat/ pique	/l/ as in lid/ needle (nēd'l)	/m/ as in mom
/n/ as in no/ sudden (sŭd'n)	/ng/ as in thing	/ŏ/ as in pot	/ō/ as in toe
/ô/ as in caught/ paw/ for/ horrid/ hoarse	/oi/ as in noise	/o͝o/ as in took	/ū/ as in cute

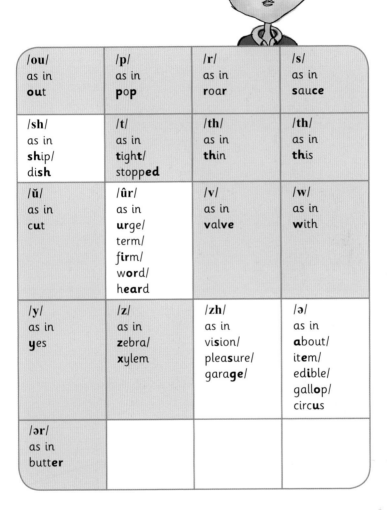

/ou/ as in **ou**t	/p/ as in **p**op	/r/ as in **r**oar	/s/ as in **s**auce
/sh/ as in **sh**ip/ di**sh**	/t/ as in **t**igh**t**/ stopp**ed**	/th/ as in **th**in	/th/ as in **th**is
/ŭ/ as in c**u**t	/ûr/ as in **ur**ge/ t**er**m/ f**ir**m/ w**or**d/ h**ear**d	/v/ as in val**v**e	/w/ as in **w**ith
/y/ as in **y**es	/z/ as in **z**ebra/ **x**ylem	/zh/ as in vi**s**ion/ plea**s**ure/ gara**ge**/	/ə/ as in **a**bout/ it**e**m/ ed**i**ble/ gall**o**p/ circ**u**s
/ər/ as in butt**er**			

Be careful not to add an /uh/ sound to /s/, /t/, /p/, /c/, /h/, /r/, /m/, /d/, /g/, /l/, /f/ and /b/. For example, say /fff/ not /fuh/ and /sss/ not /suh/.

There is a new boy in school.
His name is **Hugh**.

All the kids are excited to play with Hugh in the playground.

Still Hugh won't play. He stands alone and **doesn't** say anything.

"Maybe he's feeling blue," say the other children. "How do we get him to play with us?"

They decide the best way
is to try to amuse him.

Luke and June put on a play.
Luke dresses up as a cute

unicorn and June rides a unicycle.
Hugh doesn't say anything.

Trudy and Tallulah play a tuneful duet on the tuba and the flute.

They play the ukulele, too.
Hugh doesn't say anything.

Ruby and Judy juggle with **fruit** and play music on a huge bugle.

They dress up in matching cuddly bear **suits**. Hugh still doesn't say anything.

"What a lot of fuss for **nothing**," they fume.

"We've tried everything and he
still won't play. That's just rude."

Sue has an idea.
She goes over to Hugh.

"Hello, Hugh," she says.
"Would you like to play with us?"

Hugh says, "Yes please!"

OVER **48** TITLES IN SIX LEVELS
Betty Franchi recommends...

Some titles from Level 4

I love reading phonics — **The Circus Mice** — 978 1 84898 783 8

I love reading phonics — Monster's **Night** — 978 1 84898 784 5

I love reading phonics — **Jemima The Spy** — 978 1 84898 785 2

Some titles from Level 5

I love reading phonics — The **Gigantic Bear** — 978 1 84898 787 6

I love reading phonics — Celebrity **Celia** — 978 1 84898 788 3

I love reading phonics — The **Cemetery Dance** — 978 1 84898 789 0

Other titles to enjoy from Level 6

I love reading phonics — **Owen the Astronaut** — 978 1 84898 794 4

I love reading phonics — **Clumsy Eagle** — 978 1 84898 792 0

I love reading phonics — **Bad Zombie Movie** — 978 1 84898 793 7

An Hachette Company
First published in the United States by TickTock, an imprint of Octopus Publishing Group.
www.octopusbooksusa.com

Copyright © Octopus Publishing Group Ltd 2013

Distributed in the US by
Hachette Book Group USA
237 Park Avenue, New York NY 10017, USA

Distributed in Canada by
Canadian Manda Group
165 Dufferin Street, Toronto, Ontario, Canada M6K 3H6

ISBN 978 1 84898 791 3

Printed and bound in China
10 9 8 7 6 5 4 3 2 1